SOMEBODY
ELSE'S CHILD

SOMEBODY ELSE'S CHILD

by Roberta Silman

illustrated by Chris Conover

FREDERICK WARNE

New York · London

Frederick Warne & Co., Inc.
New York, New York

Manufactured in the United States of America
Library of Congress Catalog Card Number: 76-6780
ISBN: 0-7232-6136-9

1 2 3 4 5 6 7 8 9 10

FOR MY CHILDREN—
MIRIAM, JOSHUA, RUTH

One

When I started fourth grade, there was a new bus driver. He must have a real name, but he calls himself Puddin' Paint.

Puddin' Paint likes nicknames. The first time he saw me he said, "Hi, Smiley."

"My name is Peter."

"Well, you're Smiley to me. You've got the nicest smile I've ever seen."

Puddin' Paint wears glasses and he's older than my father, but he isn't as old as my grandfather. He's a wonderful bus driver. He never yells at us, and he knows so many songs that we sing all the way to school and all the way home. After a few weeks the people in town could hear us coming from blocks away.

I live at the last stop. I like to be the last one off the bus. Puddin' Paint sometimes lets

me turn off the motor of the bus. Then he leans back in his seat and we talk a little before he rides back to the garage—about school, or my sister Kate, or Puddin' Paint's dogs.

One day it began to snow after lunch. We had had a few flurries the week before, but you could tell this was going to be a real storm. Big, thick flakes. Soon the grass was covered, then the streets. My teacher, Mrs. Stanton, announced that there would be early dismissal. When I got on the bus, Puddin' Paint was wearing a huge fur hat with ear-flaps. The other bus drivers looked worried as I passed them. Not Puddin' Paint!

"Beautiful storm, isn't it, Smiley?" he said happily.

I nodded and sat in the seat right behind Puddin' Paint. We sang "Jingle Bells" and "Rudolph, the Red-Nosed Reindeer" on the way home.

At each stop it became harder and harder to start the bus because the snow was building up and the plows hadn't come to clear the streets yet.

"I don't know if we'll make it, Smiley," Puddin' Paint said as we started for my stop. But we did. I was disappointed. I said good-bye to Puddin' Paint and started up the hill. I listened for the sound of the engine starting. I always turned around then and waved to Puddin' Paint. I walked slowly, listening. Nothing. So I turned around. Puddin' Paint was walking through the bus.

"What's the matter?" I called back.

"The bus won't start. Maybe it's wet. I'll wait a few minutes," he told me. I went back and waited with Puddin' Paint. It was getting cold on the bus. Puddin' Paint tried again. No luck.

"Well, Smiley, I guess I'll have to go to your house and call the garage. That is, if you'll have me." Puddin' Paint grinned at me. "This bus isn't going anywhere now. And even if it did start, it's beginning to get too dangerous on these roads until the plows come through."

What a lucky break! Puddin' Paint at my house. I could hardly believe it. On the way up the hill I told Puddin' Paint who lived in each house. Finally we reached number 18. My Mom was at the kitchen window.

"Well, I'm glad to see you, Peter. Everyone else came up the hill a while ago." Mom smiled as she opened the door.

"Mom, this is Puddin' Paint."

My mother extended her hand. "I'm so glad to meet you. Peter's told us a lot about you. Will you have some cocoa? Or coffee?"

"I'd love a cup of cocoa. But first I have to call the garage. Can I use the phone?" Puddin' Paint took off his coat and funny hat.

"Of course," Mom said as she went back to the kitchen.

The garage man told Puddin' Paint he would have to leave the bus where it was until the storm was over and he would send a car around to our house for Puddin' Paint.

I went to my room to straighten my train set. I wanted Puddin' Paint to see it. It was like a miracle that Puddin' Paint was actually in our house. I could tell he liked the trains and my whole room by the way he looked at everything. Then I took Puddin' Paint all through the house.

"That was the full tour," he said.

"Cocoa's ready," Mom called.

As soon as we sat down, my sister Kate came in. She's older and goes to a different school, nearer home, so she walks.

12

"How old are you, Shining Eyes?" Puddin'
Paint said.

Kate laughed. "Thirteen."

"I told you Puddin' Paint liked nicknames,"
I said to Kate. She went to change her shoes
and socks.

"Where do you live?" my mother asked
Puddin' Paint.

"Fifteen miles north. We have a small farm
—apple orchard, vegetables, some chickens. My
wife likes that sort of thing." Puddin' Paint
smiled. "Someday you'll have to visit us,
Smiley. In the spring, when everything be-
gins to smell so good." Puddin' Paint sniffed
and closed his eyes.

Mom laughed. "Don't you like winter?"

"I love winter!" he said. "I love the snow.
Snow protects the plants and roots so they
can bloom well in the spring. Anyone who
doesn't like winter doesn't like spring. You
better believe it!"

I loved to listen to Puddin' Paint talk.

"How many kids do you have?" I asked. I
imagined a houseful, probably all grown now.
Puddin' Paint shook his head.

"No children, Smiley." He hesitated. "Well, all the kids on the bus, like you, but none of our own. We wanted some but none ever came." Puddin' Paint stood up. "Let's see if that car is coming. At this rate I'll never get home and the wife will worry."

"Do you want to call her?" my mother asked.

"No, I'll call from the garage."

There was no sign of the car. Puddin' Paint sat down again, and as Mom poured another cup of cocoa for us I was thinking. I'm adopted, and because I am I know that if you can't have a baby of your own you can adopt one. Some people might be shy about saying this, but Puddin' Paint and I are friends, so I said, "You could adopt a baby, Puddin' Paint."

He looked at me with a funny expression. "I don't think so, Smiley. We're too old now and when I was younger I didn't believe in adoption," he said. "I didn't want to bring up somebody else's child."

I swallowed hard. Mom and Kate looked at each other, but Puddin' Paint didn't notice. He was stirring his cocoa.

"Why don't you show Puddin' Paint your new caboose?" Mom said. Her voice was soft, gentle. There was still a lump in my throat so I just nodded. Then I led the way to my room.

A little while later we came back downstairs. "They sure make better toys than when I was a kid." Puddin' Paint paused. "They also make better kids. You sure made two beautiful ones," Puddin' Paint said to Mom. Then he put on his hat and coat. The car from the garage had just beeped in front of the house. Puddin' Paint tugged the earflaps of his hat down over his ears.

"Bye, Puddin' Paint," I said.

"Where's my smile, Smiley?" Puddin' Paint patted me on the head. I tried to smile but I didn't really feel like it.

"See you tomorrow—if the snow stops." Then Puddin' Paint turned to Mom and Kate. "Nice to meet you both. And thanks for the cocoa." He whistled as he walked down the snowy steps.

16

Two

We helped Mom clear the kitchen table. No one said anything. I had thought I would feel happy if Puddin' Paint ever came to visit, and I had, in the beginning. Oh, well, it didn't matter. It wasn't the first time I'd heard someone say something about adoption. Sometimes people said to my parents, "You would never know Peter was adopted, he even looks like you!" That always makes Mom mad. Those people don't understand about adoption any more than Puddin' Paint does.

Still, coming from Puddin' Paint, it hurt. It made me feel as if something was wrong with me. I started to walk back to my room. I didn't want to cry, I didn't even think I was going to cry, but suddenly there they were. Stupid tears coming out of my eyes and down my cheeks, making my lips salty.

I shut the door to my room and lay down on my bed. I pulled the pillow over my head. The tears wouldn't go away, but I felt better after I cried awhile. All by myself. In peace. My mother isn't a nosybody; she doesn't come running after you the way some mothers do when you get upset.

I started to fiddle with the train tracks. There was a knock on the door. "Can I come in?"

"Oh, O.K.," I said. I wiped my face with the back of my hand, but I knew that Mom knew I was crying. She handed me a tissue. She looked worried.

"He didn't realize you were adopted, Peter. He wouldn't have hurt you for all the world. He cares about you. He . . ."

"But he doesn't understand anything about it," I interrupted her. "He said I was somebody else's child!" I was practically shouting now. Still, she looked so calm. I couldn't understand it. Then she sat down on the bed.

"Well, that's not entirely wrong, if you want to be absolutely literal about it. You

18

know you didn't come out of me, we've talked about that."

O.K., that was true. Kate had come out of Mom and I hadn't. I came from the adoption agency. I know where it is because every year or so they have a big party there. But you don't come out of an agency, I suddenly realized. You're born.

You come out of *somebody*. You come out of your mother!

I looked up at Mom. But she looked the same. When I spoke, the words came out very slowly. "Then that means you're not my real mother," I said.

Mom shook her head. "No, Peter, I am your real mother. You came out of your natural mother. The woman who gave birth to you. But I'm your real mother and Dad is your real father. We've taken care of you since you were a tiny baby and . . ." Mom ran her fingers through the front of her hair and bit her lip. That means she's thinking.

"Look, Peter." She put her hands on my shoulders and looked directly into my eyes.

That means she's very serious and I'd better listen. "Peter, when people take care of a child the way your father and I have taken care of you, they are the child's parents. You are ours because we love you with that special love that parents have for children. No one can really describe that love, Peter."

She stopped and shrugged. "And you may not understand everything I'm trying to say now, you may have to wait a long time, maybe till you have children of your own, but believe me, Peter, you're our child, no matter who you came out of." I think she expected me to agree with her. But I couldn't. I felt confused and awful.

"But when you're born you come out of your mother," I said, and sat down next to her. My legs felt wobbly.

"Your natural mother," Mom said.

"The person Puddin' Paint called 'somebody else'?"

"Exactly."

"But why didn't she keep me? You kept Kate when she came out of you."

My mother sighed. From her face I knew I had gotten to what she calls "the heart of the matter."

"I guess that's the hardest thing to understand—for you, for Puddin' Paint, and for everybody." She frowned.

"Your natural mother, the woman you came out of—the woman Puddin' Paint called 'somebody else'—couldn't keep you. She may have wanted to, but she may not have had a home, or she may not have been married, or she may have been too young to take on the responsibility of a tiny baby." Mom stopped as if she didn't know what else to say. She looked out the window and then, just as she was about to begin again, there was Kate at the door.

"I need some help with my math," she said. "And Mrs. Winters called, and what are you two talking about for so long?" Kate's voice was whiny.

"Coming, Kate." Mom sounded tired. Then she turned to me and said, "I'll be right back. Don't go anywhere."

"I have a lot of math," Kate warned. Sometimes she's such a pest.

I tried to look at a book while Mom was gone, but I couldn't concentrate. I was really trying to imagine what it might be like not to have a home, or a room, or a backyard.

"Was she poor?" I asked my mother when she came back.

"Who?"

"My real mother. Was she poor?"

"Maybe, but maybe not."

"Then why couldn't she keep me?"

"Well, as I said before, she may have been too young to get married or to bring up a child, or she may not have been able to take care of you. Each time the circumstances are different, Peter, and I honestly don't know why she couldn't keep you. But I do know that she wanted you to have a home and a mother and a father who could bring you up. So before you were born she went to the same adoption agency we went to and told them what kind of parents she hoped you would have."

Mom's face was sad. "You know, Peter, it was probably very hard for her to give you up. But she did it because she thought it was the best for you. Not just for then or when you were a little boy. For your whole life."

I still didn't understand. "But everyone makes such a fuss over new babies, they're so cute, how could she just give me away?" I imagined a pair of hands giving me to someone like I was a package.

Mom nodded and smiled. "New babies are very cute, and so were you. But most of the time the natural mother doesn't even see the baby. Often she makes her decision before the baby is born. Sometimes the baby goes from the hospital to the people the adoption agency has picked, and sometimes the baby goes from the hospital to a temporary home for a couple of weeks and then is given to the adoptive parents. It depends on the laws of the state and the circumstances in each case. We got you when you were six weeks old."

"I thought it was six and a half weeks." It was Kate, listening at the door when no one wanted her.

24

"What do you want?" I said.

"To come in."

Mom laughed. "Well, that's honest! Can she come in, Peter?" I shrugged, and before I could open my mouth she was sitting on the rug. Sometimes I don't even get a chance to talk, and I couldn't say *get out* now, so there she was—just sitting there.

"Can I tell about the day he came?"

"In a minute. First I want to tell Peter again what was happening around here before he was born," Mom said.

"While your natural mother was telling the people at the adoption agency what kind of parents she hoped you would have, we were talking to them, too. And telling them we had tried and tried to have another child and nothing was happening. So since we couldn't have another child of our own we wanted to adopt a baby."

I could tell from the expression in my mother's eyes that she was remembering. "You know how it feels to wait for something. It was only a couple of months, but it felt like years! Then one day the agency called and said they had a baby boy for us. And soon after that we had two children— Kate and Peter."

Mom and Kate looked perfectly normal, but I felt all clammy again.

"It's better to come out of your mother," I blurted. "It's simpler."

26

My mother sighed again. "I suppose it is. I know it is. But I also know, Peter, that some things aren't simple, even some of the best things that happen to us."

She didn't seem to know what else to say, so we just sat there for a few minutes, the three of us. Then Mom hugged me to her. "It's a lot to take in at one time, Peter. That's why so many people don't understand adoption and say awkward things about it." She hesitated. I knew she was thinking about Puddin' Paint. Then she said, "We'll talk again soon, but now we'd better go into the kitchen so I can start dinner. Dad will be home soon."

Back in the kitchen I heard about my first night home. I had heard some of it before, but Kate had to tell it all the way through. Girls are like that.

"First you spit up your bottle, then you cried for hours, and then you spit up your bottle again. And then," Kate grinned at me, "you were so sleepy that you slept the whole next day, which was Saturday, and Mom got so scared she called the doctor."

"Even though Dad told me not to," my mother added.

"And the doctor came," Kate continued, "and told us you were adjusting and absolutely fine, and he had really sick children to visit."

"Of course I felt like a fool," Mom said. I laughed. Then Kate and I set the table. I stood at the front window and watched the snow coming down. Across the street some kids were trying to make a snowman. I didn't even feel like going out. It was cozy in the house.

But after Dad came home and we had had dinner, I felt like playing in the snow. Dad turned on the big outside lights, and Kate and I made snow angels and snowballs and started the base for a fort. We could see Mom and Dad talking at the dining room table. I had the feeling that Mom was telling Dad about what Puddin' Paint had said. It was strange, but somehow I wasn't mad at Puddin' Paint. It was like Mom said. Adoption is hard to

understand, and Puddin' Paint had probably never tried to understand it. Maybe someday I could tell him about it, I thought.

Kate and I smoothed the sides of the fort. Then Dad came out to fill the bird feeders, and Kate had to go in to do her homework. I was lucky that night—I didn't have homework—so Dad and I walked down the hill to see if the school bus was still there.

"What a night!" Dad said. "Look, the bus is gone. The plows must have been through. I guess you'll have school tomorrow, Peter."

I nodded. "I hope Puddin' Paint got home O.K.," I said, and we walked slowly back up the hill.

Three

Puddin' Paint had gotten home fine, and the next day the bus came as usual.

"What a nice mother and sister you have, Smiley!" Puddin' Paint said. "And if you want the best cocoa in the world you should go to Smiley's house," he told the rest of the bus. For the next few days our house was full of kids taking Puddin' Paint's advice.

More snow came. And more, and more. Over the Christmas holidays the kids on the block picked up Kate and me almost every day and we went skating and sledding and made a huge snow fort. Then, suddenly, on New Year's Day it was as warm as spring. The melting snow made little streams in the streets. You didn't even need a jacket!

"I hope you kids don't catch colds," Mom said with a little frown as we walked through the slush to a neighbor's. We groaned.

31

"Well, you're not wearing a jacket, either," Kate said.

"No," Mom said, smiling. "It's incredibly warm."

The warm weather kept up. When I got on the bus the first day back to school, I was sure Puddin' Paint would have something to say about the "January thaw," which is what my parents called it.

But Puddin' Paint was very quiet. He barely smiled at any of us. He seemed very tired.

He looked the same on the way home. At the end of the ride I waited a bit until the bus was empty. Then I said, "Do you feel O.K., Puddin' Paint?"

He jumped a little. Then he turned toward me. "Oh, it's you, Smiley." He tried to smile. "No, I guess I don't feel O.K.," he said. I was afraid he was going to tell me something had happened to his wife or his farm. My hands got all tingly.

"My dogs are gone," Puddin' Paint said. "Disappeared on New Year's Day. I guess the

32

warm weather went to their heads. They just ran away. They've never done that before. I was feeding the birds and one of those small private planes flew quite low over our land. It isn't the first time a plane has done that, but this time it seemed to scare them, and the dogs took off. Didn't listen at all. Just took off and kept running, and by the time I went back to get the car they were out of sight."

Puddin' Paint held his forehead as if he had a headache. "The wife and I have spent the last three nights and days looking for them. I haven't slept much."

I wanted to say something that would make him feel better, but I didn't seem to be able to find the words.

"Well, I'd better be getting along," he said. "We have more searching to do."

He sounded so tired. Not plain tired, but what my Dad calls 'worried-tired.' "I hope you find them," I said.

"So do I. My wife's beside herself. Those dogs are like kids to us, you know."

"What are their names?" I suddenly realized Puddin' Paint had never called them by name, just "the dogs."

He looked a little embarrassed. "Kind of funny names. Black and Brown. Nothing very exciting, but we got them when they were pups and we called them that in the beginning just to tell them apart. The names stuck."

"They're nice names," I said. "I sure hope you find them."

Puddin' Paint shrugged, then waved, and I started up the hill.

When I got into the house Mom asked, "What's the matter, Peter?"

"How did you know something was the matter?"

She smiled. "I watched you come up the hill. You walked so slowly and your head was down. Whenever you walk with your head down something's the matter. When you were little and unhappy you used to crawl with your head down. You looked like a turtle."

I started to laugh, then I remembered and

frowned. "Puddin' Paint's dogs ran away on New Year's Day. He's spent the last three days and nights looking for them. He looks so tired."

"Who's tired?" It was Kate.

"Puddin' Paint. He lost his dogs." I told her the story, and later, at dinner, I told Dad how tired and upset Puddin' Paint was.

That night I dreamed about Puddin' Paint. I kept hearing "Black? Brown? Black? Brown?" in my sleep. Suddenly my mother was there. "Hush now, hush," she said as she covered me. I opened my eyes.

"You were having a bad dream, Peter. You were shouting: 'Black, Brown, Black, Brown,' " she told me. She didn't seem to know what was going on, and I was too tired to explain.

The next morning the sun shone very bright, but it was winter again. The thaw was over, and frost covered the grass and made designs on the windows.

It was freezing on the way to the bus. The cold seemed to go through everything. The

minute I saw Puddin' Paint's face I knew that the dogs were still gone.

I kept thinking about Puddin' Paint all through school. We don't have a dog because Kate is allergic, but I tried to imagine what it would be like to have to search and search for something you loved.

"Peter, what's gotten into you today? This is the third question I've asked you that you can't answer." Mrs. Stanton said, "Do you feel all right?"

"I'm O.K.," I said, then listened a little harder so I was able to raise my hand with the answer a few minutes later.

As the class was lining up for the buses I thought about Puddin' Paint again—how lonely he must feel, how discouraged.

On the bus I sat right behind him. I could see his face in the mirror. He didn't even look like himself. I felt I had to help him, so when the bus stopped I said very quickly, "Puddin' Paint, can I come home with you and help you look for Black and Brown?"

Puddin' Paint smiled, then shook his head.

"Thanks, Smiley, you're really a good kid to want to help, but God knows when I'll get back, probably long after you're supposed to be asleep." When Puddin' Paint looked at me I knew he would have taken me if he could. Right then, I made a decision.

"If Black and Brown aren't back by Saturday can I come then?" I said in a loud voice, because I expected a no.

But Puddin' Paint surprised me. "Sure, Smiley, that is, if it's O.K. with your Mom and Dad." He scratched his head and looked out the window. "But I sure hope those dogs turn up before then. It's getting colder now."

Each day I hurried to the bus stop and each night I told Mom and Dad and Kate that the dogs were still gone and that Puddin' Paint was getting more and more discouraged.

On Friday they were still gone.

That night I asked if I could go out with Puddin' Paint on Saturday to look for the dogs.

Mom and Dad looked at each other.

"We scarcely know him," my mother began

slowly. "And you'd be driving around all day." They don't like me to drive with just anybody.

"But I drive to school and back with him every day," I said. They smiled at each other. That encouraged me.

"I'd really like to help Puddin' Paint," I said. "He's so worried now that it's cold again."

"It's supposed to be freezing tomorrow. They predict a record, down to zero the radio said." Mom frowned.

"I think we could bundle Peter up and let him go. We can call Puddin' Paint now and tell him, and I'll drive Peter there in the morning." Dad turned to me. "We'll come for you at suppertime." I was so happy, I felt like I had the best father in the whole world!

I laid out my warmest shirt and my long underwear and ski pants. The next morning Dad and I had a big breakfast together while Kate and Mom slept late. It was only seventeen degrees and the predictions were for the temperature to drop to record cold. "But

40

it's clear and dry, and you're lucky there's no wind," Dad said as we drove.

Puddin' Paint was waiting for us. He had a big bag of sunflower seeds in his arms. "I've just filled the feeders," he said as he shook Dad's hand. "The birds are ravenous. There's a thick crust of ice over everything. It's so hard for the animals to find food when it's this cold." I knew Puddin' Paint was thinking about Black and Brown.

We went inside. Puddin' Paint's house was exactly what I expected—small and neat and smelling of hot biscuits. It must smell good like that every day. Puddin' Paint's wife was also small and neat, and she smelled of clean wash. She insisted we taste her biscuits.

"These are the best biscuits I've ever eaten," I said and licked my fingers. She was pleased.

"I put some in your lunch, Peter," she said kindly. I liked her face, but I could see that she was tired and worried, too.

"Aren't you coming?" I asked her.

"No, not today. I've got to get this house

cleaned up and some cooking done. I've been out looking for the dogs so much that I've got lots of catching up to do."

Dad said he would be back for me around suppertime. Then he left, and we got into Puddin' Paint's station wagon. There were heavy wool blankets in it. Puddin' Paint's wife gave us a big knapsack filled with sandwiches and three thermoses of cocoa.

"If it gets too cold, stop somewhere and warm up," she warned. "It's going to be terribly cold."

Four

I liked being alone with Puddin' Paint. The warm car was like a cocoon that protected us from the cold. The snow that had fallen during the night glared in the bright sunlight. I had to close my eyes to keep them from getting watery while I talked to Puddin' Paint.

"Where are we going?"

"There's a spot about fifteen miles away that borders the big state park. I used to take the dogs there fishing. I went there the third day we were looking, but it started to rain so we didn't get as far as the lake." Puddin' Paint pulled down the window visor. "There, now you can open your eyes, Smiley," he said.

When I did I could see that his face was worried. "Everything's turned to ice," he said with a frown. "If we don't find the dogs today they're going to freeze to death." He really loved those dogs. He would do anything for them, I thought.

He seemed able to read my mind.

"Those dogs mean a lot to us, Smiley." He looked down at me. "When you've had animals since they were pups, well, they get into your bones. They become part of you." He stared straight ahead the way people do when they're afraid they are going to cry.

"The way kids do?" I asked softly.

"I guess. I guess so."

I started to understand what Mom had been trying to tell me the other day. About the love parents have for children. If Puddin' Paint loves his dogs this much then imagine how much Mom and Dad care about Kate and me. Mom was right. You can't really describe that. I was getting a feeling for what she was talking about, and right then I knew I had to tell Puddin' Paint I was adopted. I'm not sure why it had to be then. It isn't the sort of thing you can lead up to, so I just said, "I think you ought to know I'm adopted."

I thought he would be surprised, but he took off his cap and slowed the car down a little and looked at me. "I kind of suspected that the day I came to your house. You all got very quiet when I said I didn't believe in adoption. And on my way home I realized that I didn't know anything about it and I had just blown my mouth off."

"That's O.K., Puddin' Paint," I said.

"I felt bad then, Smiley, and I'm sorry now. I want you to know that."

"I do," I said, and for a while there wasn't anything to say.

After about a half hour we came to a town, well, not really a town, just a clump of houses.

"This must be one of the smallest villages in the state," Puddin' Paint said. "It has a post office and a grocery and a vet. They say he's a good vet, too. But I never understood how he could stay in business in this little place." Puddin' Paint shook his head. "Years ago there was more farming around here, before the state bought most of the land for a park."

46

A few people were walking on the road. An old man in a red hat waved, then soon we were all by ourselves again. More snow had fallen up here. The trees glittered, the woods were so still. Occasionally a white-tailed rabbit hopped across the road, which was getting bumpier and bumpier.

Suddenly the car lurched to a stop.

"Road ends here," Puddin' Paint said. "We'll have to walk from now on."

I pulled on two pairs of mittens and my hat that looks like a mask. I had thought Mom was crazy when she insisted I take this hat, but now I was glad to have it.

Puddin' Paint pulled down the earflaps on his fur hat and reached for the knapsack. Then he rolled the two blankets together, tied them up and lashed them to the knapsack with a long rope. He put the whole thing on his back. I knew that the blankets were for the dogs if we found them.

Our feet scrunched the crusted snow as we walked. "It's almost a mile from here," Puddin Paint said. He kept looking down on the ground for paw prints, he said, so I did, too.

47

"Deer droppings," he said occasionally. Our breath misted across our faces. I could feel my ears stretching toward some sound, any sound really, but mostly the sound of a dog barking. All we could hear was our own feet.

We neared a widening in the path. "Well, here's the lake," Puddin' Paint said. The lake was frozen. He looked at his watch, then walked over to a rock and brushed the snow off it.

"Come on, Smiley, time for some food. We don't want to freeze to death."

The cocoa felt so good going down, and the biscuits were still warm. Puddin' Paint handed me a sandwich.

"I'm not that hungry after the biscuit," I said.

"Better eat it anyway. When it's this cold you need a lot of fuel to keep that fire going." Puddin' Paint was right. I felt warmer after I ate the sandwich.

"I don't know whether to turn around, or take the path into the woods at the north end of the lake," Puddin' Paint frowned. "I have

48

this nagging feeling that those dogs are some-where in those woods."

"Let's take the path then."

"It'll be a longer walk back," he warned.

"Oh, don't worry about me," I said.

For safety's sake we walked around the lake instead of across it. "You never know, and all we need is to fall in. That would top every-thing," Puddin' Paint said.

The path from the lake was narrower and rockier than the one we walked on before. It wasn't so silent, though.

"More animals live here. There's a salt lick a few miles away," Puddin' Paint said over his shoulder. We had to walk single file in lots of places.

Suddenly he stopped and walked off the path. "Look," he said, pointing to some drop-pings. "That's not deer, that's a dog." Puddin' Paint dug his hand into his pocket and pulled out a compass. I watched him sight it, then we started to walk. I was getting used to the cold now, so I rolled back the mask part of my hat. A little later there were some more droppings.

"I may be crazy, but let's call," Puddin' Paint said.

We began. "Black, Brown, Black, Brown." Then we stopped shouting and walked some more. "Black! Brown! Black! Brown!" we called again. Nothing.

Then I put my hand on Puddin' Paint's arm. "Wait a second," I whispered. I thought I heard something way off in the distance.

"Did you hear anything?" he said.

"I thought so, something little. Did you?"

Puddin' Paint shook his head. "No, but you have younger ears. Let's walk a little further and call again."

The next time I was sure I heard it. Puddin' Paint still didn't hear anything. "Which direction, Smiley?"

I pointed. "That's more northwest." Puddin' Paint sighted the compass. "Well, let's give it a try."

We walked for several minutes. There were no more dog droppings; I began to think I had made a mistake. Puddin' Paint stopped. "Let's stand very still and call and see what happens." He cupped his hands around his

50

mouth, and I did the same. "Black, Brown, Black, Brown!" we called and waited. In the distance there was a thin thread of sound.

"Did you hear it?" I said.

"That time I did." Puddin' Paint bent his ear toward the sound. We were almost running. I had to be careful not to slip on the thin sheet of ice that covered the rocks.

We called again. The same thin thread-like sound answered.

"I'd swear it was miles away from the sound of it, but then they couldn't hear us." Puddin' Paint scanned the woods. "They both have such big barks when they want to," he added.

"But if they're hurt?" I asked.

He nodded. "Let's keep moving." He hunched his shoulders, sighting the compass again.

Suddenly, a low whimpering sound floated toward us. I leaned toward it. "You lead," Puddin' Paint whispered.

We were in a thicker part of the forest, evergreens surrounded us. I had to push away the branches to get through. My eyes were watery from the cold. I blinked a lot, it was hard to see. But then I saw something red.

"Look!"

We ran toward the dogs. They were caught in two animal traps that had been set side by side. The snow around them was stained with blood.

Puddin' Paint's face was grim as he approached the dogs. Their legs were tangled in the traps, their eyes glassy, they scarcely looked alive. Black was deeper in his trap than Brown. It was Brown who had whimpered.

"We've got to work fast," Puddin' Paint said. Quickly he unrolled the blankets and opened the knapsack. "Here, hold this." He gave me a cup, then filled it with cocoa. "Try Black first." But the dog couldn't even drink. He looked at me and seemed to shake his head. I gave the cup to Brown. He lapped it up, but very slowly. Puddin' Paint was unpacking a small wrench.

"Good dog," he said. "Now Smiley, I'm

going to try to release these traps, but it's
tricky. They're not made to get these animals
out alive. You stand back."

It seemed like hours while Puddin' Paint

worked on the releases. There was a trickle of blood from both dogs the whole time. I was sweating all over. Brown had stopped whimpering.

"Now," Puddin' Paint's voice was tense. "I think this'll do it. God, I hope so." You could feel the silence pressing all around us. Then, with a snap, Black was free. But he didn't even move. He just lay there. After a few minutes Puddin' Paint got Brown out. He couldn't move either.

"We'll have to make a stretcher with the blankets and carry them to the car." Now I knew why Puddin' Paint had taken so much rope. Quickly we wrapped the blankets around the rope, then Puddin' Paint pulled some diaper pins from his pocket.

"I've been carrying these around with me all week but I didn't think they'd be hurt like this. Just cold, or very hungry." He pressed his lips together, his mouth was a thin straight line across his face. Then he shook his head like he couldn't believe all this was happening.

Five

We carried the dogs back to the car on the homemade stretcher. At one point I was sure my shoulders would break. Just then Puddin' Paint said, "Want to rest?" But I shook my head. How could we stop when Black was bleeding to death?

Back at the car Puddin' Paint made a tourniquet out of two old towels for each dog. As he was tying Black's leg up, the dog's eyes rolled back; he was unconscious. I kept watching to see if Black's chest was moving as we rode back to the village.

"I sure hope that vet is there," Puddin' Paint said as we got into the car.

When we got to the village, it looked like a ghost town. Puddin' Paint frowned. He pulled up at the grocery store and jumped

out. The store looked closed. But the door was open. He went in.

He came back quickly. "The grocer's the vet!" he shouted. Behind him was the old man in the red hat. They pulled the stretcher out of the back of the station wagon.

"Round the back," the old man said. The blankets were dripping blood. I ran behind them. An old woman was holding the door open.

"Why, you're just a little boy!" was all I remembered hearing. Later they told me I had fainted.

When I woke up I was on a funny-shaped couch in a very odd kitchen. It was filled with books and papers and plants, as well as pots and pans and dishes. A door at the far end of the large warm room was open. I could see a table with Brown on it. But it was Black I was worried about.

"Here, son." The round old lady blew on a spoon and held it up to my mouth. I swallowed some soup. It was thick and good. I could hear the vet's voice. "The black one will probably have a limp, but he's lucky to be alive. The brown one will walk just fine." I closed my eyes. Both dogs were alive!

When I opened my eyes again, the lady was smiling and handing me another spoonful of soup. I heard the vet's voice again.

"They're darned lucky you found them when you did. A few more hours and they would have both been dead."

Then I heard Puddin' Paint's voice. "I

didn't find them, the boy did. He heard Brown whimper. It was the tiniest sound you can imagine. I still don't know how he heard it, but he did."

Then I realized that the vet's office was the room attached to the kitchen. When they came into the kitchen, Puddin' Paint rumpled my hair a little. "Well, hello, Smiley, feeling better?"

"What happened?" I asked.

Puddin' Paint explained, "You were so exhausted that the minute you hit the warm kitchen you just fell over. Then you opened your eyes and said, 'I'm so sleepy,' and went to sleep." I smiled, but I felt like going to sleep again right then.

"That was about a one-and-a-half-mile walk back to your car, if you were where I think you were," the vet said as he lit his pipe. It had a nice smoky smell.

"And those dogs weigh about thirty pounds apiece," Puddin' Paint added. He smiled at me.

"You should be mighty proud of your son," the old lady said. She kept spooning more

60

soup into my mouth. I didn't really want it, but I didn't know how to tell her that.

Puddin' Paint winked at me. "Oh, Smiley's not mine. He has two handsome young parents. But you know, I wish he was ours. With a son like old Smiley here, well, you'd have nothing in the world to worry about." A shiver went down my spine. I leaned back on the pillows. All I wanted to do was sleep. But Puddin' Paint said, "Say now, Smiley, don't go back to sleep. Everyone's already getting worried, I'm sure. We're late right now."

I looked out the window. The sky, the trees, the snow all had a purplish hue, the sun was almost down. "What time is it?"

The old man answered. "Don't know exactly, son. We don't have a clock. When you get to our age you don't need clocks, or phones, either."

"Come on, Smiley, time to go," Puddin' Paint said.

"Not till he finishes his soup," the old lady said. I felt like I was floating as I put on my shoes. I started to tell her how light-headed I felt, but she said, "There now, save your strength, son."

62

I ate the rest of the soup and then, while Puddin' Paint and the vet carried the dogs to the car she insisted I eat a piece of her home-made raisin bread with butter. It was good, but I was already full. I felt stuffed when I started to walk.

The old people stood at the door while we walked to the car. I had to lean on Puddin' Paint because my legs felt so funny.

"Bye, good-bye," they called and waved. As we drove off into the peaceful sunset I could hear the even breathing of both dogs. They were already fast asleep.

I must have fallen asleep, too, because the next thing I heard was my Dad's voice.

"We were beginning to think about calling the police," he said to Puddin' Paint as he carried me to the farmhouse.

"Well, the roads were icy up north and I had precious cargo here," Puddin' Paint said. I could see that it was after seven on the kitchen clock. Dad called Mom on the phone, and when I spoke to her I could tell that she had been worried, too. Her voice was all tight. While we had dinner I wished that my mother and Kate were here. Over dessert I said so.

"They'll come for dinner very soon," Puddin' Paint's wife promised.

And you know what? She kept her promise. Two weeks later we all went back. It had snowed again and everything looked beautiful. Believe it or not, Black and Brown were playing in the snow. Black still had his cast on, but both he and Brown played fetch with Kate and me. And Kate didn't sneeze. Not once.

Who knows? Maybe now we can get a dog.